BALDERDASH

BY
STEPHEN E. COSGROVE

ILLUSTRATED BY ED GEDROSE

GRAPHIC ARTS CENTER PUBLISHING COMPANY

International Standard Book Number 1-55868-045-4

Library of Congress Number 91-71068

Text © MCMXCI by Stephen E. Cosgrove

Illustrations © MCMXCI by Ed Gedrose

Published by Graphic Arts Center Publishing Company

P.O. Box 10306 • Portland, Oregon 97210 • 503/226-2402

President • Charles M. Hopkins

Editor-in-Chief • Douglas A. Pfeiffer

Managing Editor • Jean Andrews

Designer • Becky Gyes

Color separations and stripping • Wy'east Color, Inc.

Typographer • Harrison Typesetting, Inc.

Printed and bound in Hong Kong

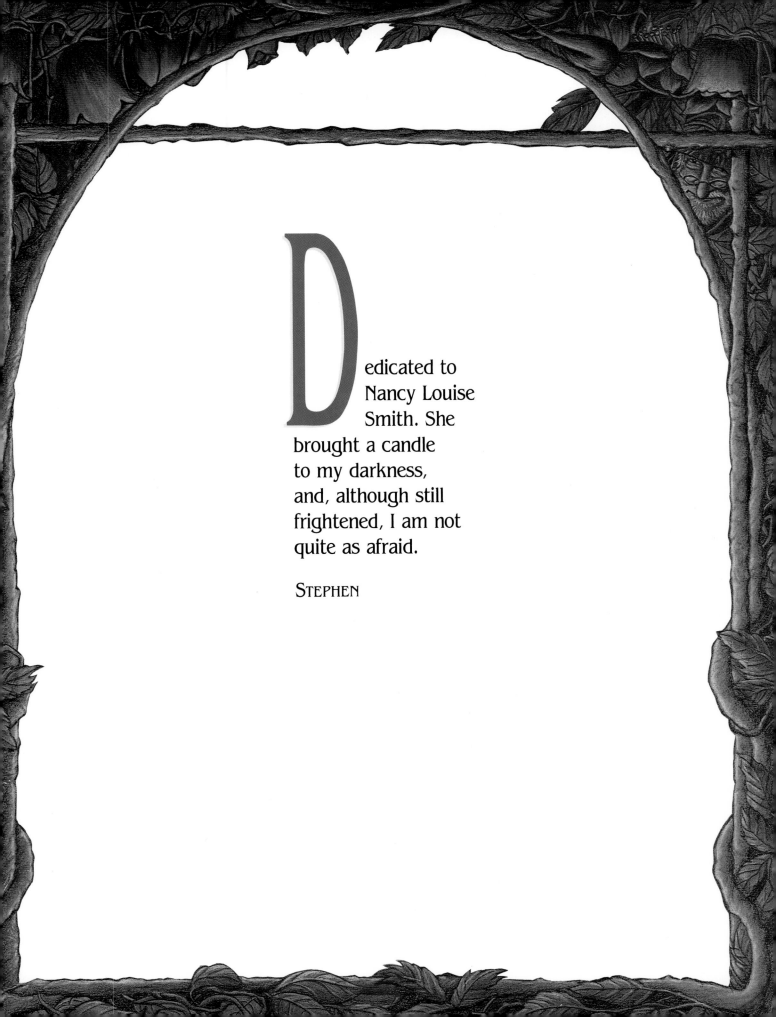

Dedicated to Nancy Louise Smith. She brought a candle to my darkness, and, although still frightened, I am not quite as afraid.

STEPHEN

olden ribbons of light lanced through the piney boughs illuminating a forest glade. These shafts of light and bright streaked through the bower and bracken shining on flower, mushroom, and garden path.

Beyond the lighted path and slightly past this brightly hued garden of roses were the shadows. Washed first in a lack of light and nightly drenched darker later, this was a very scary place indeed. Knee-high blankets of fog waited to wrap around innocent walking legs. Here, hiding, were twisty-snakes and skittering things. Shaded shapes of black and gray wisped and whisked as they peeked, primed to scare wit and wisdom from those not strong enough to hold onto them.

This was the land of Bugaboo where scary things didn't wait for the dark of the moon. In daylight shadows deep they leaped—velvet silhouettes that lunged and plunged about in this gloaming. The border between frightened and downright scared was nothing more than the vague line between bright sunlight and shadowy black.

Look, there in the border! Even now creatures are skittering about, lurking, looking for someone to scare.

4

Oh, and it was here in this land of Bugaboo that lived the fairies—wood sprites if you like. They were a tiny folk who dressed in natural things: clothes woven of cotton and Irish moss. Loosely woven skirts of leaves and hammered-bark vests hung loose on tiny-wiry frames while on their heads and 'round their necks they often wore crowns of purple-kings thistle, rosemary and thyme—amulets and lucky charms.

These were very superstitious wood sprites, and they were superstitious by chance, not choice. For, you see, the sprites were afraid of any kind of dark and all that lived in the shadows. Unfortunately, the garden where grew all of their vegetables was only in full sunlight for moments at a time between shadows, and that time wasn't enough to seed, weed, and harvest. They worked as quickly as they could, but as shadows reached stealthy fingers into the light, they retreated, very hungry, but much more afraid.

So afraid were the wood sprites of all that might be in the shadow, they would rather go hungry than be caught in the sticky web of their own imagination. Their quarter-moon eyes darted about, looking out for this or for that.

Frightened as much as some and a little less than others was a pretty little fairy called Velvet Rose. She sat wrapped in her hooded cloak on a moss-soft log as the flames of the nighttime fire launched festive sparks that rocketed up into the starlit sky. Velvet Rose sat, watched, and listened this night like any other night as sprite after sprite told scary stories of the creatures that scuttled about the shadows of Bugaboo.

Now there is nothing wrong with telling scary stories of wishes and witches as you sit about a blazing fire. But it is one thing to tell a story; it is quite another to believe it. The wood sprites believed any and all stories. The more they believed, the longer the daylight shadows became and the less bright-light time they had to gather nuts, fruits, and berries. Every day there was less and less to eat.

Velvet Rose realized all this as she sat near the fire, her stomach growling in hungry protest. Finally hunger won over fear and she vowed that come the next morning she would seek out the monsters of the shadows and tell them of the sprites' plight. Surely, upon hearing how hungry they were, the shadow creatures would allow extra light to spill into the forest, giving the sprites longer to harvest their crops.

The very next day, as the morning light caused the misty creatures to skitter back to the shadows where they belonged, Velvet Rose woke resolved to her destiny. She quickly dressed and 'round her neck she placed a necklace of mistletoe and baby's breath to wrap her in the protection of love. Over her shoulders she tossed a cape to warm her from the dankness of the shadows deep.

Dawn was a brave time to start an adventure of this sort, for shadows are always at their weakest in the light of morning bright. Armed only with her sharpened sword of hunger, Velvet Rose dashed down the path of primrose and rushed to the garden. Much to her chagrin, the garden was still covered in crooked, shadowy fingers that nearly reached over the path.

"Oh, dear," she whispered as she wrung her hands in despair, "they're in there, the monsters are. I just know they are."

If not for hunger, Velvet Rose would have never stepped into the darkened bracken, let alone crossed the shadowed path. But hungry she was, and braver she became. So, though little armed, she took a tiny step into the inky blackness.

She stood there, one foot cold in shadow, the other warmed by the morning sun. "Hmm," she said, bolstered by her bravado, "my foot's still there, and nothing has eaten me yet. Maybe I am yet to go farther."

Boldly now, she stepped full into the shadow and was swallowed whole by all that her mind had made. Oh, yes, and the monsters were there—sprite brutes of every sort. There were switch witches—bundled bunches of branches and brambles. There were shadow bats hanging upside down as they leered at Velvet Rose and her fertile imagination. Everywhere she looked there were twisted mist monsters and ogres of indescribable body bearing. Oh, it was most frightening, and she would have run, save for the fact that her feet seemed frozen to the ground and refused to listen to her pleas to leave.

There she was, trapped in the darkest shadows of Bugaboo.

But, you know, an odd thing happened that day. Velvet Rose found that the shadow creatures were not quite as scary as she had at first imagined. Slowly, she turned her head and noticed that the shadow monsters were hardly acting the part as they hobbled about whispering to one another and pointing blackened drip-draped fingers at her. "Ahem," she said, "and uh, well, how do you do?"

At the sound of her voice, the creatures jumped back, and there came a quaking sound like leaves rustling in the wind. Finally, one of the bundled switch witches clacked forward and crackled, "What do you want?"

"Want?" Velvet Rose nervously asked. "What do I want? Why I want more sunlight in the garden."

"We can't do that," snapped the witch.

"Why?" asked Velvet Rose, just a little afraid.

"Because only the shadow king can," all the creatures moaned. "The shadow king, Balderdash who lives in the Grotto—where the sun never shines!"

"Then, I am off to the Grotto," retorted Velvet Rose. As an afterthought, she turned as she left and shouted, "Boo!" Those creatures of shadowed night tumbled over one another in fumbling fright.

Now, the Grotto was a dark place in the land of Bugaboo, darker than any shadowed shade or cloudy, moonless night. This cave, this cavern, was a place where the sun had never shone and light had never entered. Sculptured shrubs twisted in anguish as they tried to reach or be touched by the sunlight that never came. Roses, daffodils, and daisies all had gone to seed 'round its shaded entry—wild and barren with neglect.

It was here that Velvet Rose came, for all who had listened to campfire stories knew that the worst of your fears always lived in dark, dank grottoes and caves. She boldly walked to the edge of the sunlight and peered into the gloom. "Halloo . . . alloo . . . loo . . . ," her voice echoed, "is there anybody there? . . . there? . . . ere?"

The only answer was the wet sound of water splashing a drip at a time forebodingly into stilled puddles. Then, as if from the bowels of the earth itself came a horrible howling, "Ooooo!! Cooome innn froom the light, sprite!"

Velvet Rose's eyes snapped open wide, and she screamed, "Oh, Lordy. Get going feet, don't worry about me. Save yourselves!"

Velvet Rose ran as fast as her little legs could carry her. With her cape whipping behind, she ran and she ran and would have run completely out of this story, save for the fact that she was still just as hungry as could be. She puffed and panted in a patch of sunlight near the edge of the garden. "Oh, that was so scary!" she wheezed. "I thought I was caught for sure."

"Caught by what?" asked the other wood sprites, who had been timidly trying to work in the garden.

"Why, Balderdash," she answered, "the king of all the shadow monsters. He nearly caught me in the Grotto."

"Ooh," they said in awe and with not just a little bit of fear. "Don't ever go back there."

Velvet Rose was just about to agree when she realized that she was still very hungry indeed. "Oh, dear," she sighed, "I must go back and tell Balderdash of our plight. Surely then, he'll allow us more light."

With feet dragging in the dust of the trail, she reluctantly went back to the Grotto. Step by agonizing step, she forced herself back to face her fears. She was nearly there when her eyes lit up like candles on a birthday cake. "I must go to Balderdash to ask for more sunlight, but there's no reason I can't take a bit of light with me."

With that, she dashed into the forest, brushing through two or three shadow shapes and paying them no mind whatsoever. Once into the forest, she found a branch of Pitchey Pine that had fallen to the ground. With this club in hand, she retraced her steps to the path and now with a bolder stride headed for the Grotto. Along the way, she knelt to pick up one of the bits of flint, hard silica rock, that were strewn about the path.

It wasn't a moment after she returned to the Grotto that the horrible howling began again from deep inside, "Ooooo!! Cooome innn from the light, sprite!"

"Is that you, Mr. Balderdash, your highness, sir?" she called nervously from the entrance. "I don't suppose that you would coome heere?"

There was a long pause from inside the cave, and naught could be heard save the incessant dripping of water. Then the silence was broken yet again, "What?" the monstrous voice asked incredulously, "You want me to . . . what?"

"Uh, I just wondered if you could come to me in the sunlight."

"Noooo!" he roared, "I am the great and wizardous Balderdash, shadow king of all that is scary, skitters, or scurries in the dark. Why would I come to you?"

"I don't know," said Velvet Rose, "I just thought maybe it would have been polite if you had come to me."

Two solitary drips dropped loudly into puddles deep within the cave, and then the shadow king roared even louder, "Well, I am not polite . . . I am Balderdash, and don't you forget it, you not very bright sprite."

Velvet Rose had been called many things in her life, but she had never been called dumb. "Well that's just fine," she snapped. "You are the rudest brute I have ever met."

"Well, what did you expect," muttered the shadow wizard from the inky blackness of the Grotto, "peanut butter and jelly?" There was a long pause, and finally Balderdash called again from the shadows, "Ooooo!! Cooome in heere from the light, sprite!"

"Oooo, Oooo," saucily retorted Velvet Rose, "Your mother must have been a nightmare."

"You leave my mother out of this, you . . . you sputtering sprite!" rumbled the monster.

Well, Velvet Rose was beyond fear now; she was mad. She was really mad, for she never sputtered at all. She carefully laid the branch of Pitchey Pine on the ground and struck flint to rock. Tiny sparks flew from the edge of the rock until one little spark landed at the top of the branch and began first to smolder and then burst into flame. She lifted the branch high into the air and watched happily as the shadows leaped back into the depths of the cave.

"Here I cooome!" she bravely taunted.

Velvet Rose's footsteps echoed loudly in the cavern as torchlight played off the puddles, shooting reflections in every direction. With every step, the torch lit up more and more of the dark and mysterious Grotto. Oddly enough, the Grotto didn't seem quite so frightening in the light with the shadows gone.

There was a rustling at the back of the cave, and Balderdash nervously called out in his blustery voice, "What did you just do?" For as much as the sprites were afraid of the dark, so was Balderdash afraid of the light.

"You wouldn't come out into the light, so I thought I would bring the light to you," said Velvet Rose as she boldly hopped between the puddles.

There was another mad scurry, and then Balderdash nervously laughed, "Well . . . well, hee, hee, hee. Let's not be hasty. I mean . . . well . . . why are you here? I mean . . . what can I do for you, little fairy?"

Velvet Rose kept moving, swinging the torch from side to side, as she spoke, peering into the gloom, "I came first to the monsters that lived in the shadow to ask if they would give us more sunlight to work in the forest, but come to find out, they weren't so scary. They sent me to you, but you won't come out into the light."

"Well," said Balderdash, closer now and very frightened as Velvet Rose and her lighted torch reached the back of the Grotto, "I grant thee thy wish . . . 'poof' . . . you now have more sunlight. Now, please go."

"Well . . ." said the little fairy, "I guess if you promise not to scare any of the wood sprites in the garden anymore, I'll leave." Once again she squinted in the dim light to catch a glimpse of this creature of fright, but the most she could see was a long, distorted shadow that flickered and danced upon the glistening walls of the cave.

"Oh, yes . . . yes . . . yes. I promise," said Balderdash as he tried to hide from the flickering light. "No problem, ha, ha! Yes, siree. There will be no more scaring sprites in Bugaboo."

Satisfied that all would be right from that moment on, Velvet Rose turned and left the Grotto and the very frightened wizard within.

It took a while for all the sprites of Bugaboo to understand that their fear of the shadows was unfounded. But in time, they found the shade to be just that, a cool place to sit on a warm summer's day as they rested from their work in the forest. And in the shadows, too, Balderdash found that light was not as frightening as it seemed. There he taught the sprites to make shadow puppets of light and bright.

If you're afraid at night
of the shadows that fright,
seek them in the light of day.
You'll be more than surprised
as you realize
that monsters of the mind
are really sort of kind
when you find them alone in the shadows.

Other books in the DreamMaker Classic series:

THE
DREAM
STEALER

PRANCER

The
TERRY BROOK
DRAGON

™